A BASKETBALL

FULL-COURT DRAMA

text by Dionna L. Mann • art by Oscar Herrero

PICTURE WINDOW BOOKS
a capstone imprint

Published by Picture Window Books, an imprint of Capstone
1710 Roe Crest Drive, North Mankato, Minnesota 56003
capstonepub.com

Library of Congress Cataloging-in-Publication Data
Names: Mann, Dionna L., author. | Herrero, Oscar, 1973- artist.
Title: Full-court drama : a basketball graphic novel / text by Dionna L. Mann ; art by Oscar Herrero.
Description: North Mankato, Minnesota : Picture Window Books, [2024] | Series: Slam dunk graphics | Audience: Ages 5-7 | Audience: Grades 2-3 | Summary: Aiden wants to win at basketball, so when rookie Chloe joins the team he becomes frustrated she is not perfect, but he soon remembers what it means to be a supportive teammate.
Identifiers: LCCN 2022062270 (print) | LCCN 2022062271 (ebook) | ISBN 9781484680582 (hardcover) | ISBN 9781484680537 (paperback) | ISBN 9781484680544 (pdf) | ISBN 9781484680568 (kindle edition) | ISBN 9781484680575 (epub)
Subjects: CYAC: Graphic novels. | Basketball—Fiction. | Teamwork (Sports)—Fiction. | LCGFT: Sports comics. | Graphic novels.
Classification: LCC PZ7.7.M33447 Fu 2024 (print) | LCC PZ7.7.M33447 (ebook) | DDC 741.5/973—dc23/eng/20230404
LC record available at https://lccn.loc.gov/2022062270
LC ebook record available at https://lccn.loc.gov/2022062271

Designed by Dina Her

Printed and bound in China.   5557

MEET THE TEAM

Aiden loves basketball and winning. He's a skilled player.

Coach Matt leads the Panthers basketball team. He wants them to work together.

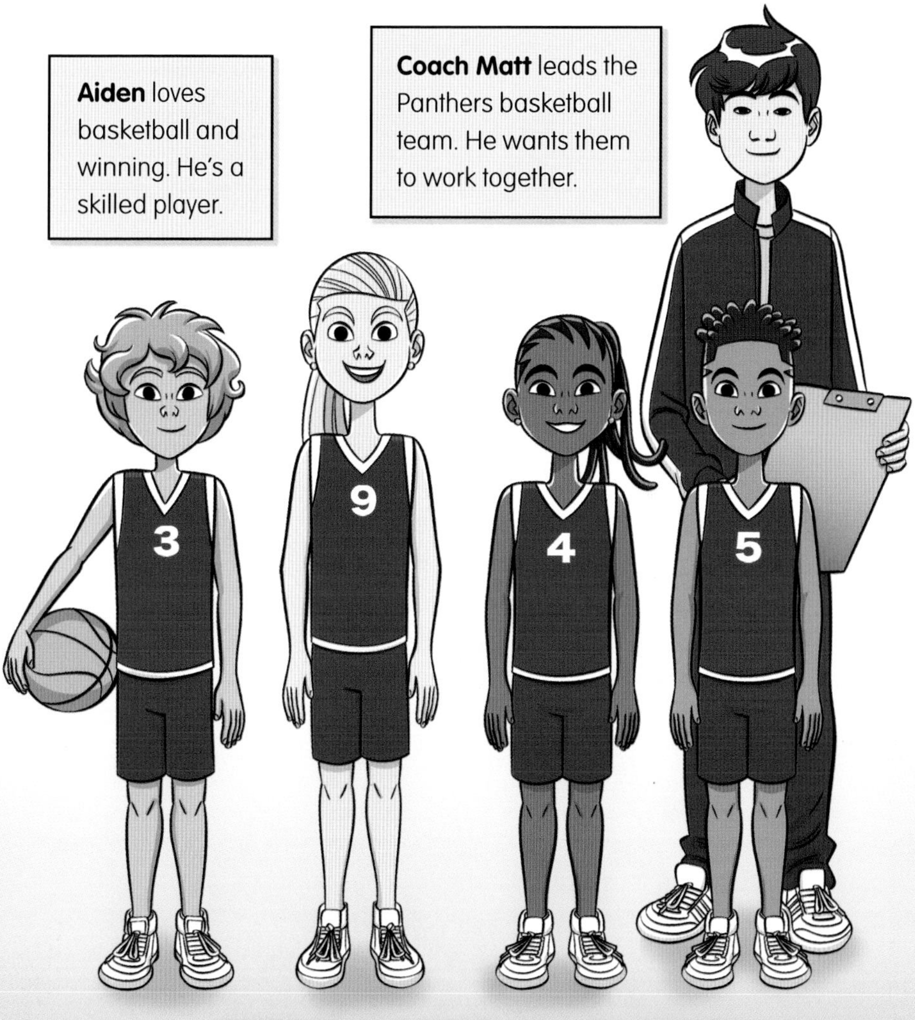

Chloe is new to the Panthers. She's new to basketball too.

Lyra and **Cooper** are Aiden's friends. This is their second year on the team.

HOW TO READ A GRAPHIC NOVEL

Graphic novels are easy to read. Boxes called panels show you how to follow the story. Look at the panels from left to right and top to bottom.

Read the word boxes and word balloons from left to right too. Don't forget any sound and action words in the pictures.

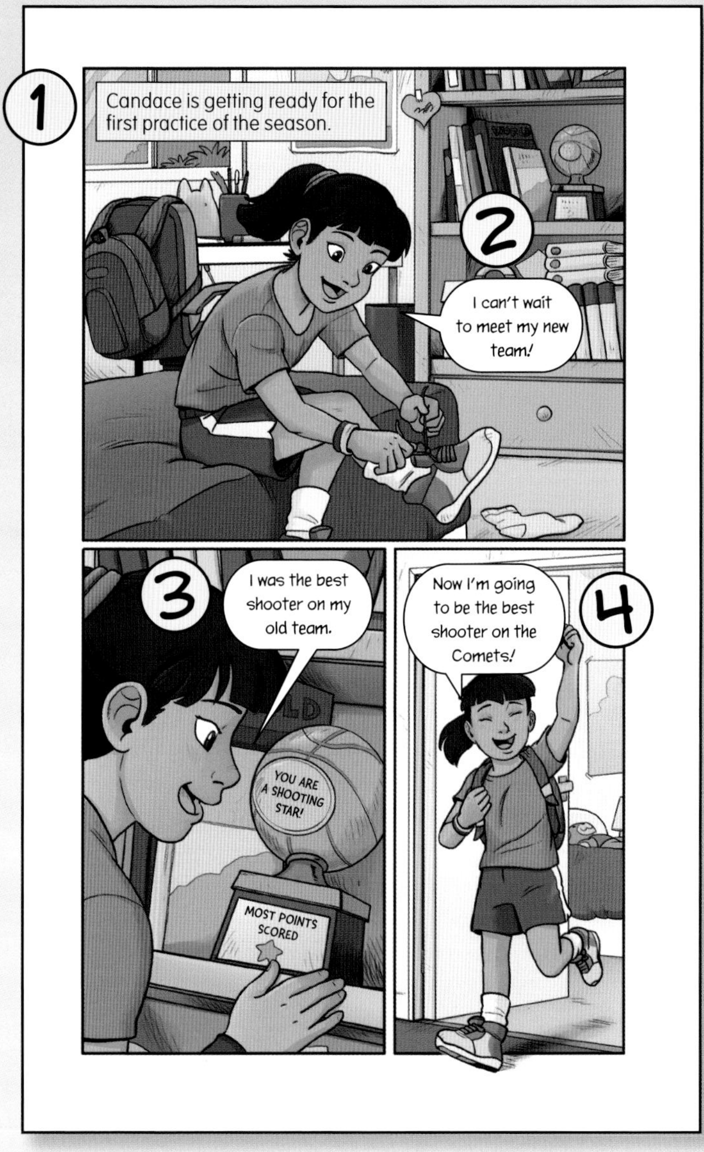
1
Candace is getting ready for the first practice of the season.
2
I can't wait to meet my new team!
3
I was the best shooter on my old team.
YOU ARE A SHOOTING STAR!
MOST POINTS SCORED
4
Now I'm going to be the best shooter on the Comets!

All the pictures and words work together to tell the whole story!

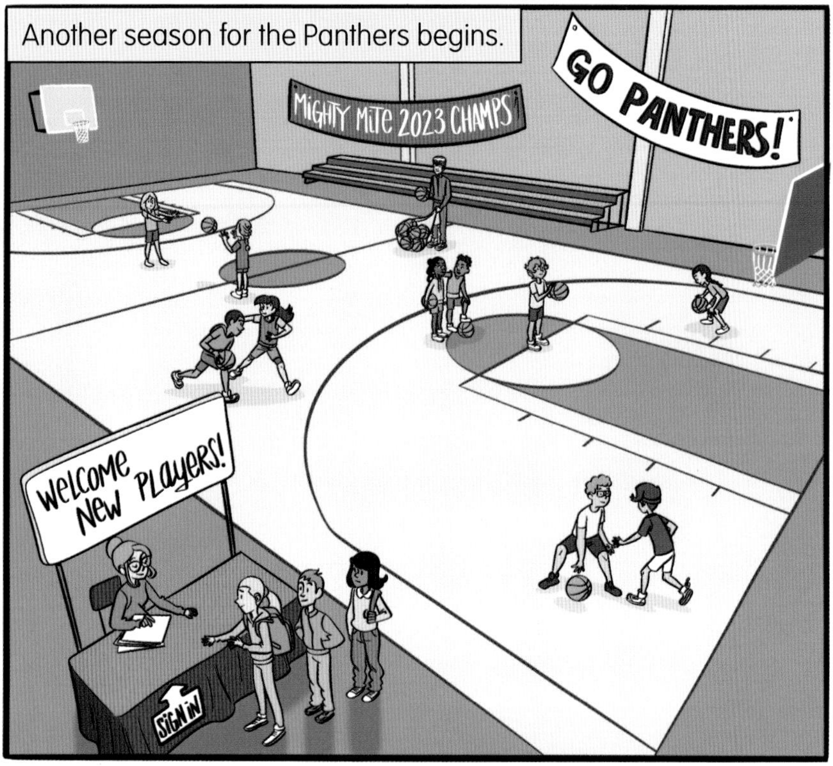
Another season for the Panthers begins.
MIGHTY MITE 2023 CHAMPS
GO PANTHERS!
WELCOME NEW PLAYERS!
SIGN IN

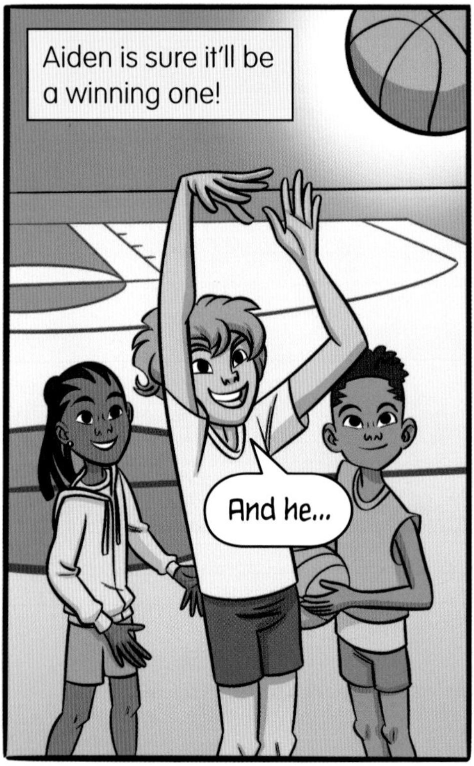
Aiden is sure it'll be a winning one!
And he...

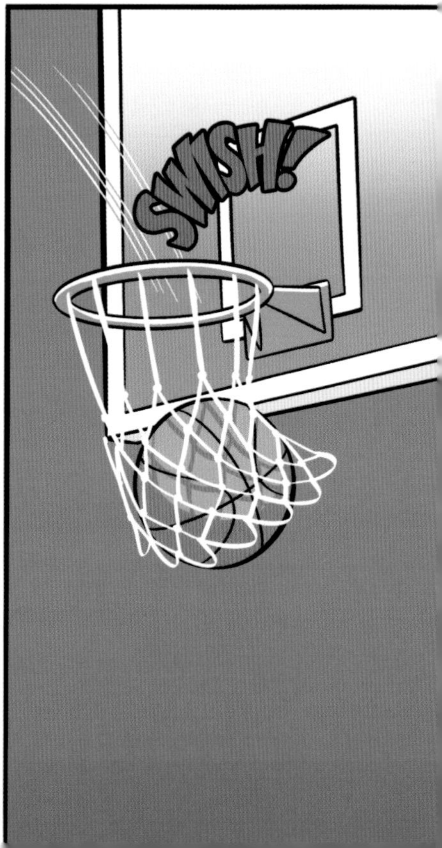
SWISH!

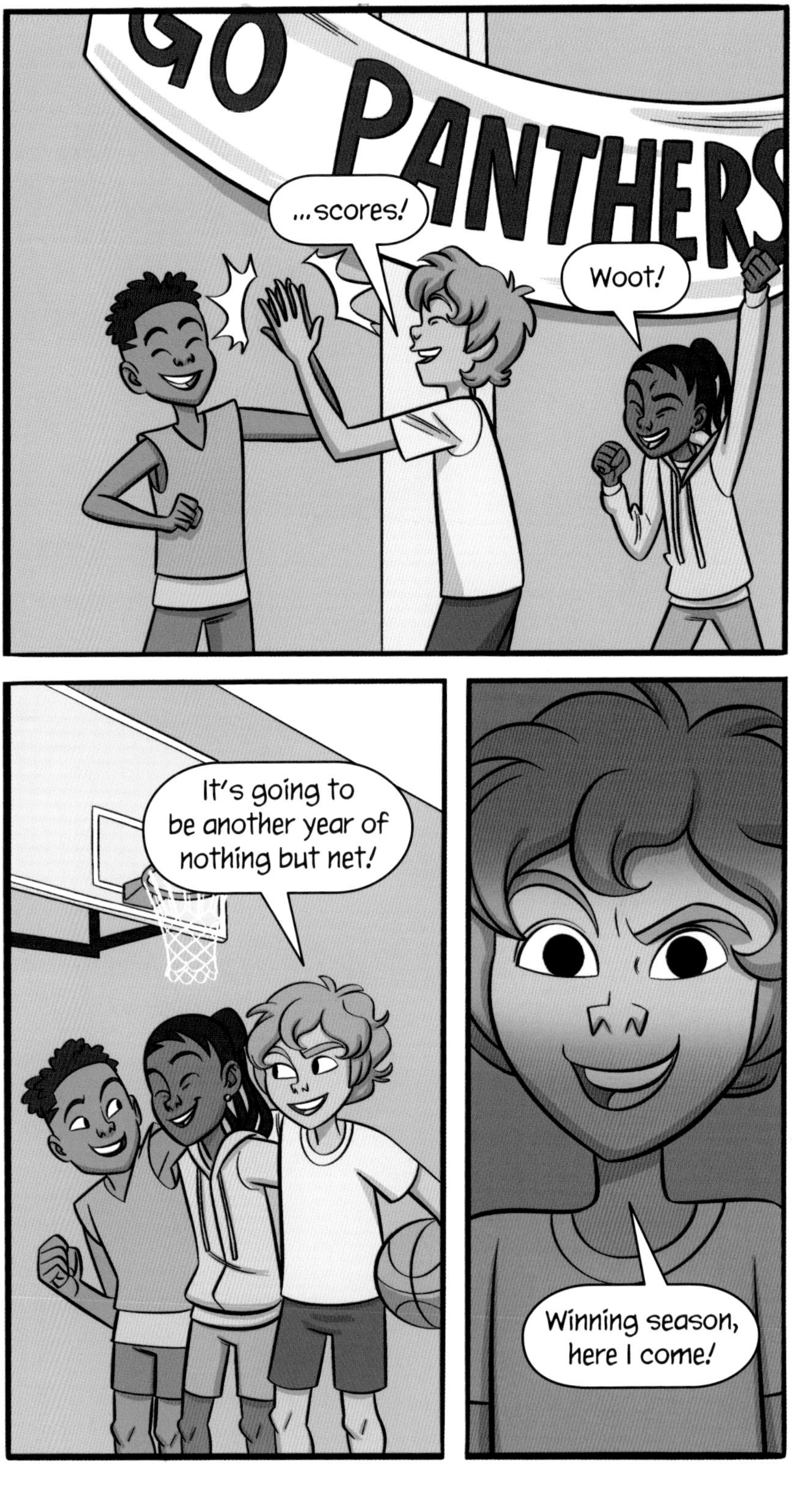
GO PANTHERS
...scores!
Woot!
It's going to be another year of nothing but net!
Winning season, here I come!

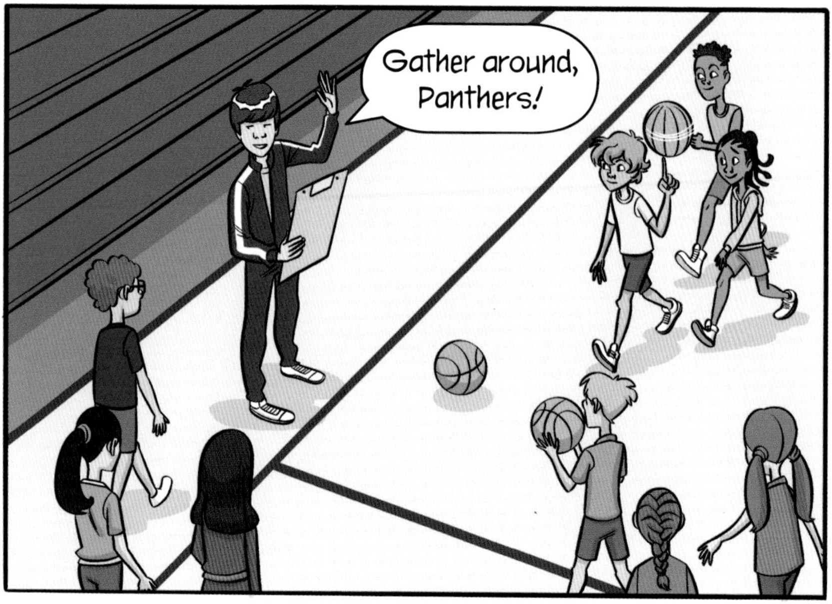
Gather around, Panthers!

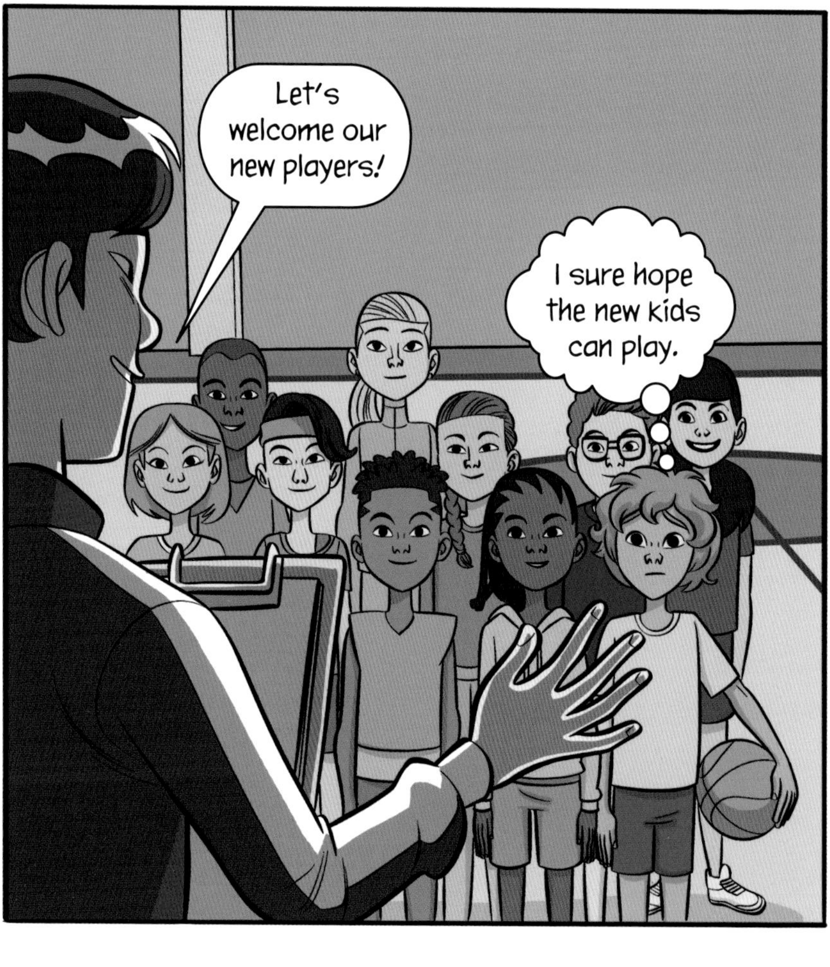
Let's welcome our new players!
I sure hope the new kids can play.

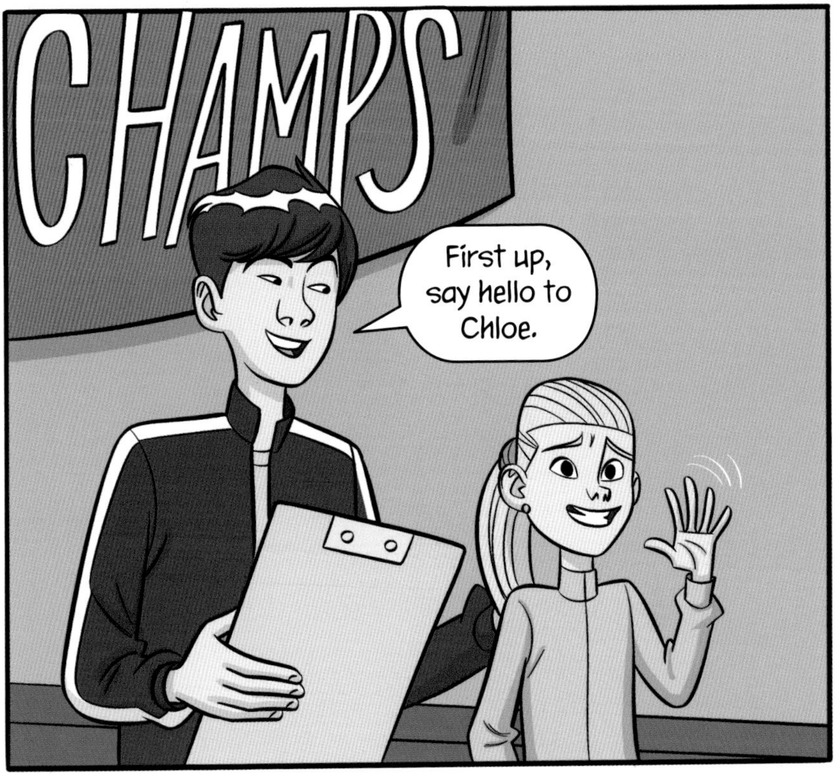
CHAMPS
First up, say hello to Chloe.

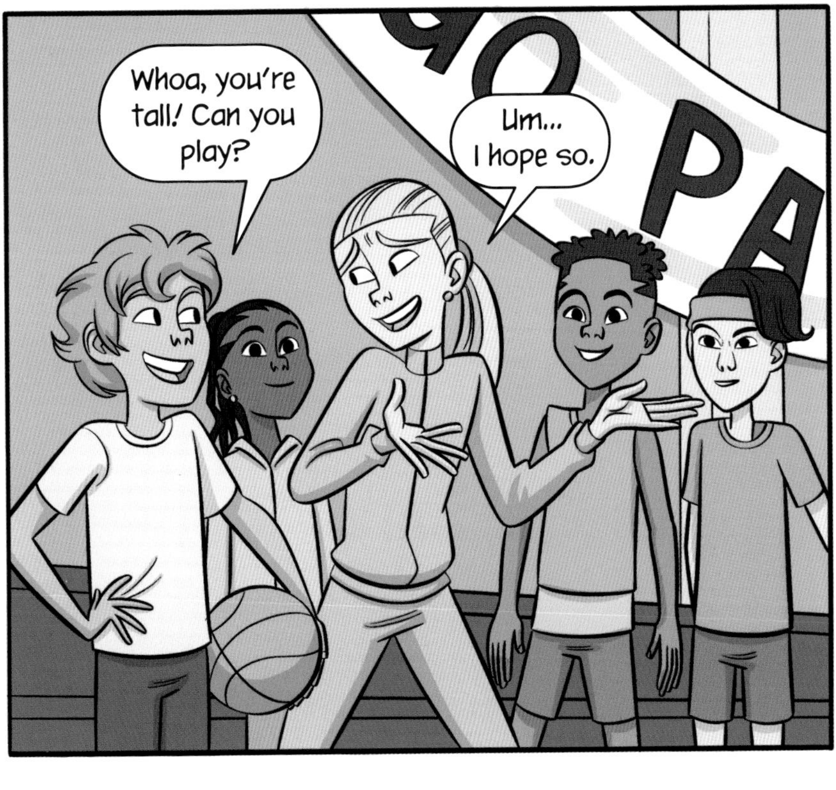
Whoa, you're tall! Can you play?
Um... I hope so.

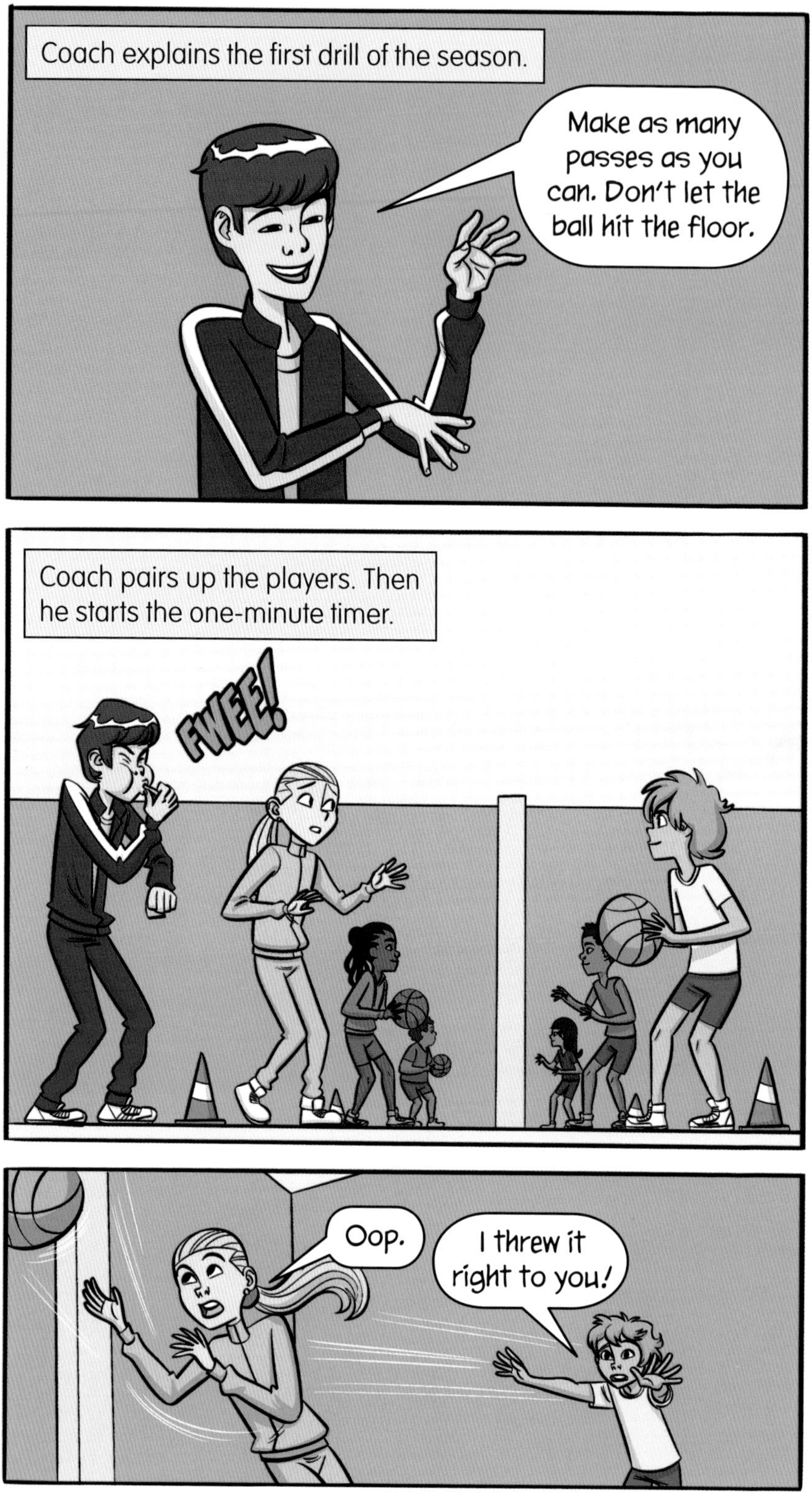
Coach explains the first drill of the season.
Make as many passes as you can. Don't let the ball hit the floor.
Coach pairs up the players. Then he starts the one-minute timer.
FWEE!
Oop.
I threw it right to you!

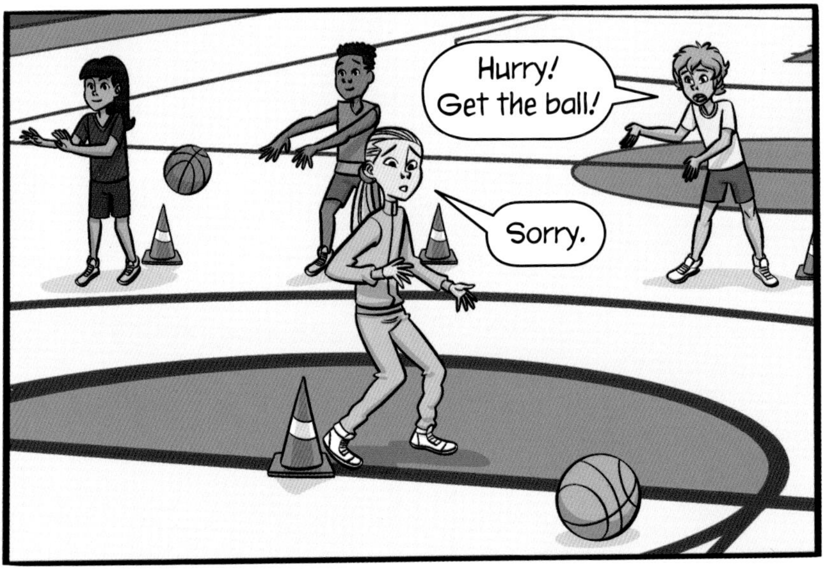
Hurry!
Get the ball!
Sorry.

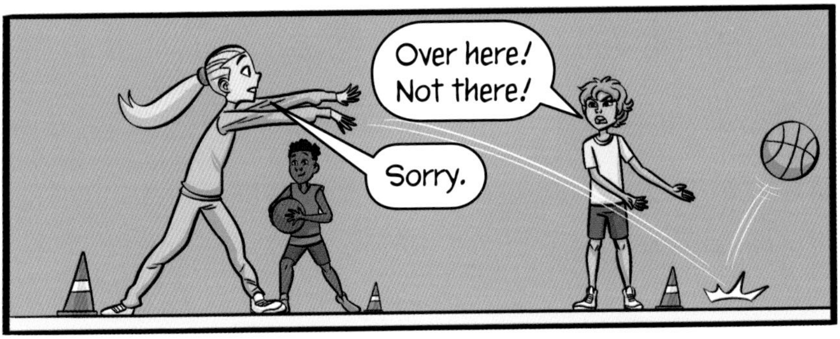
Over here!
Not there!
Sorry.

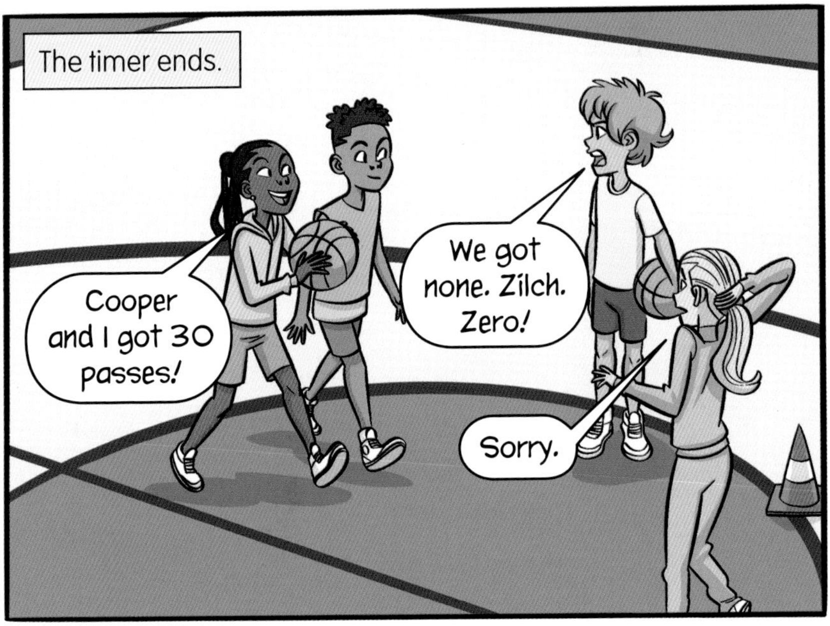
The timer ends.
Cooper and I got 30 passes!
We got none. Zilch. Zero!
Sorry.

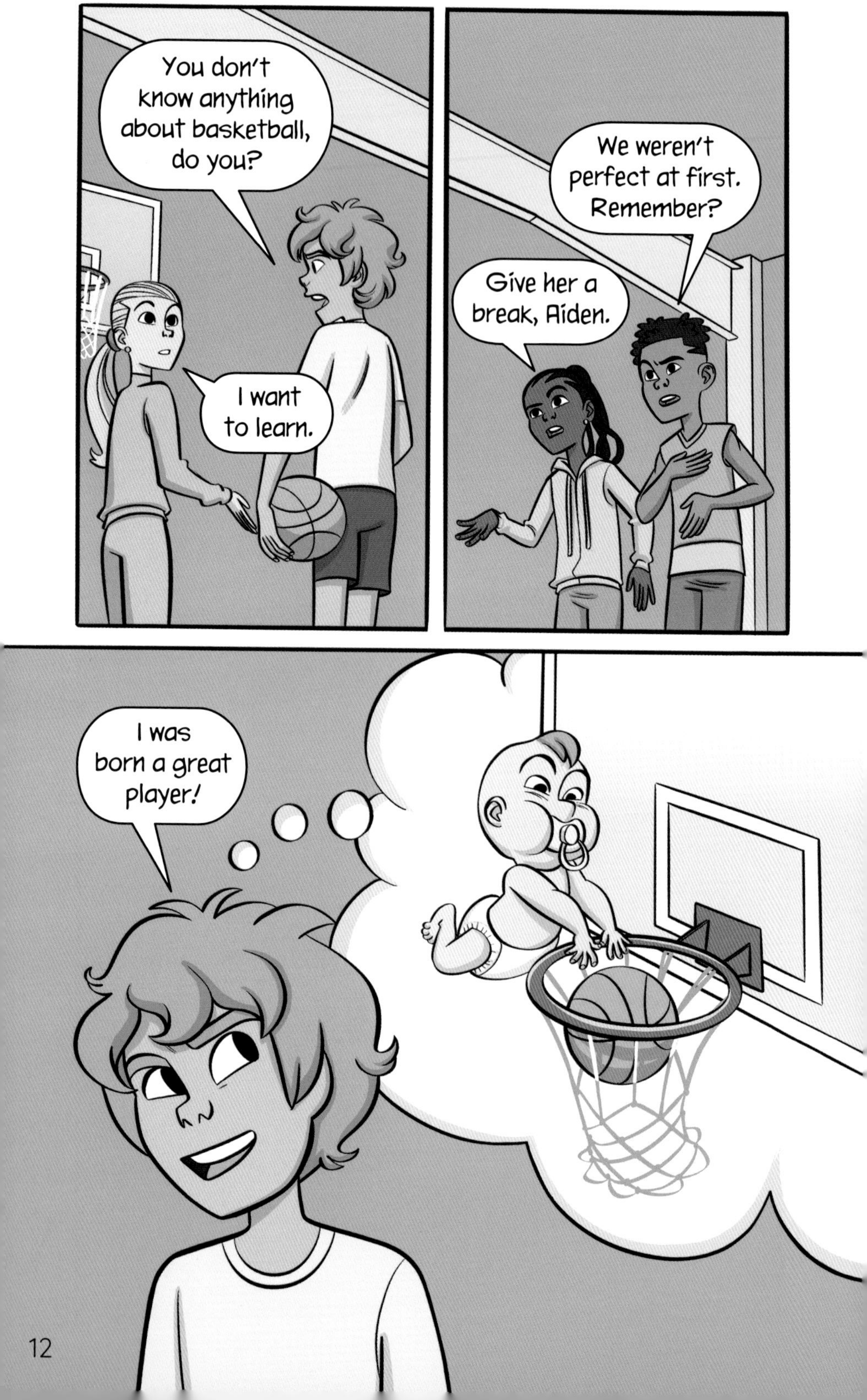
You don't know anything about basketball, do you?
I want to learn.
We weren't perfect at first. Remember?
Give her a break, Aiden.
I was born a great player!

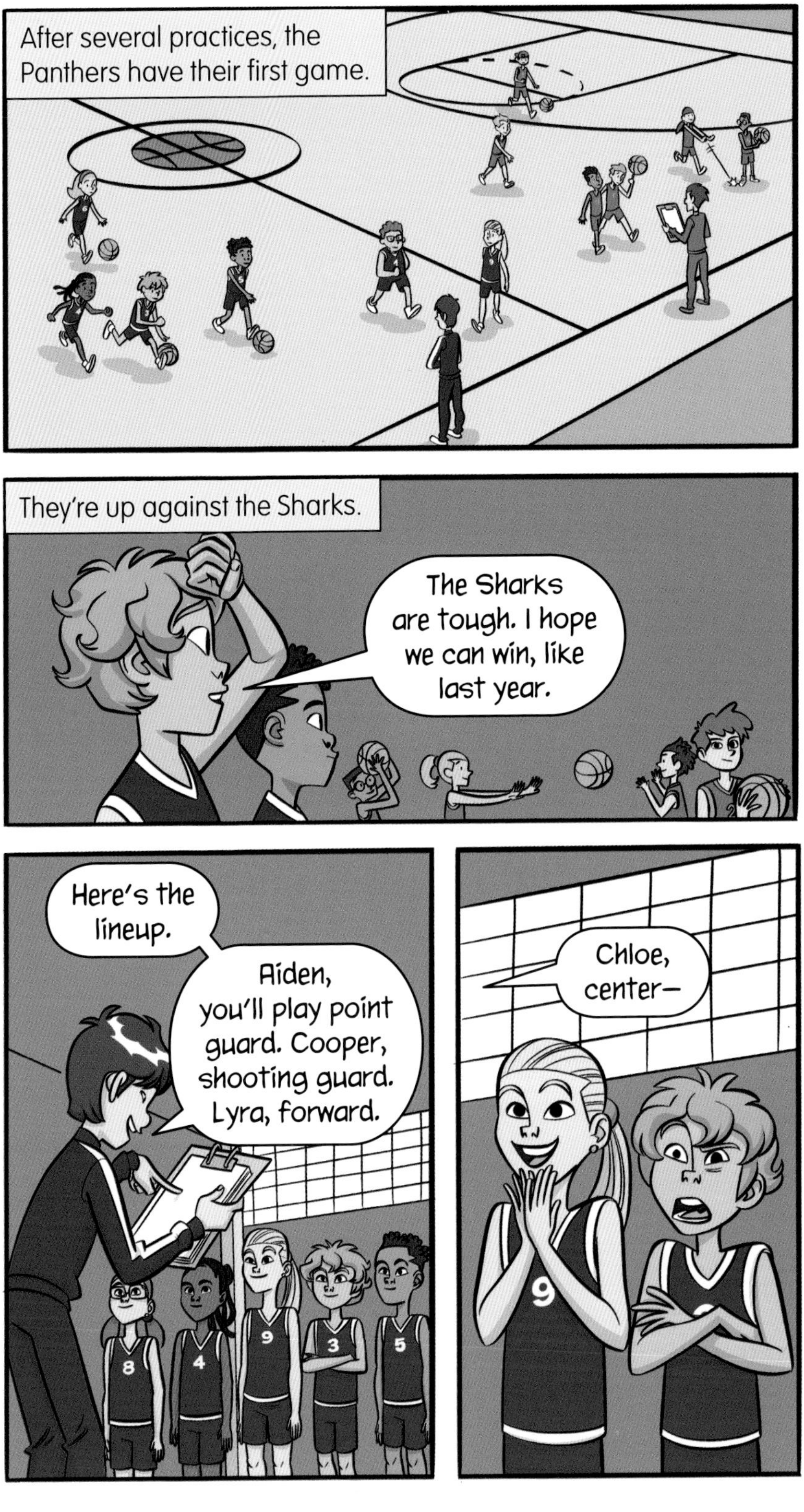
After several practices, the Panthers have their first game.
They're up against the Sharks.
The Sharks are tough. I hope we can win, like last year.
Here's the lineup.
Aiden, you'll play point guard. Cooper, shooting guard. Lyra, forward.
Chloe, center—

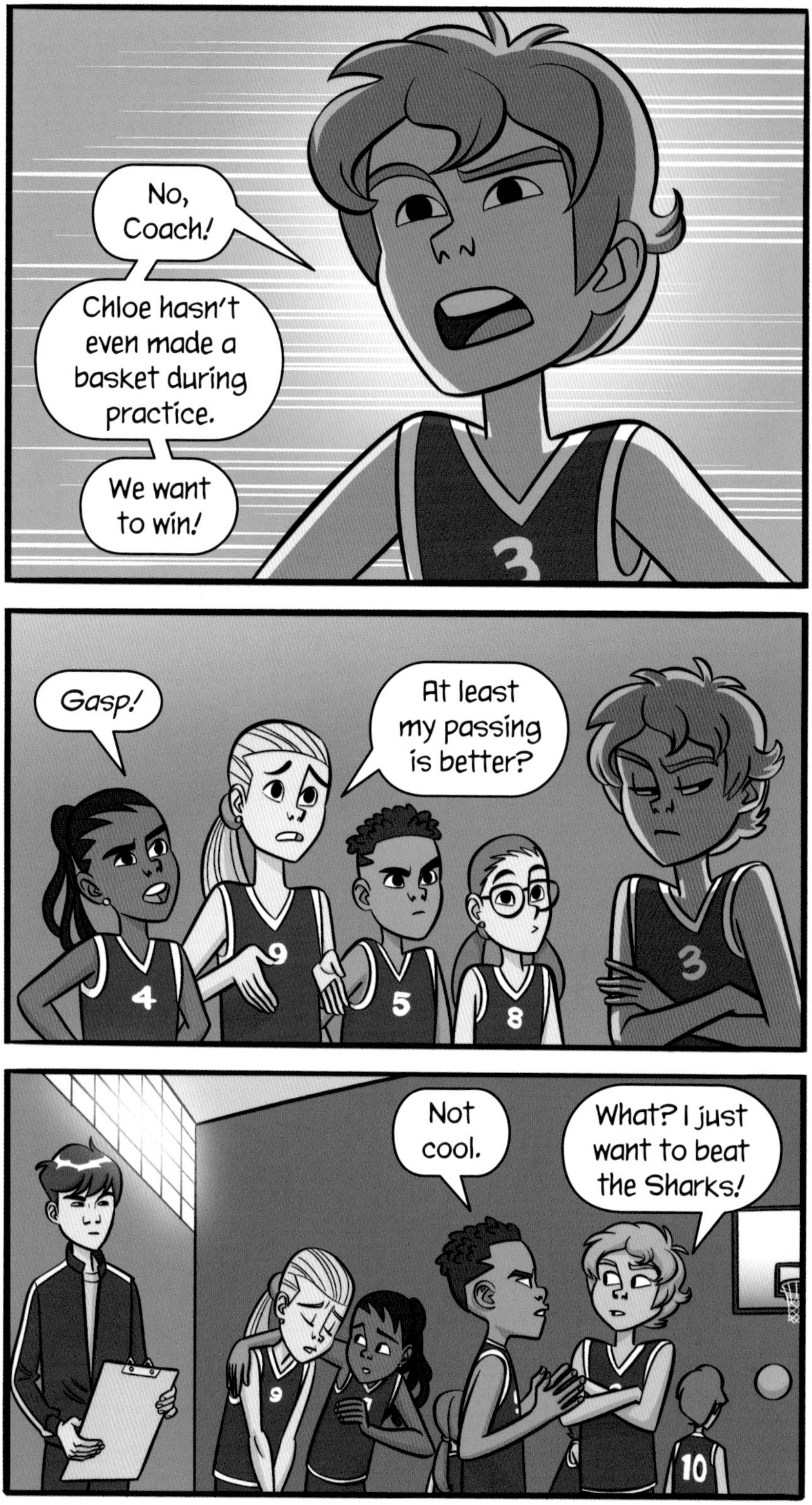
No, Coach!
Chloe hasn't even made a basket during practice.
We want to win!
Gasp!
At least my passing is better?
Not cool.
What? I just want to beat the Sharks!

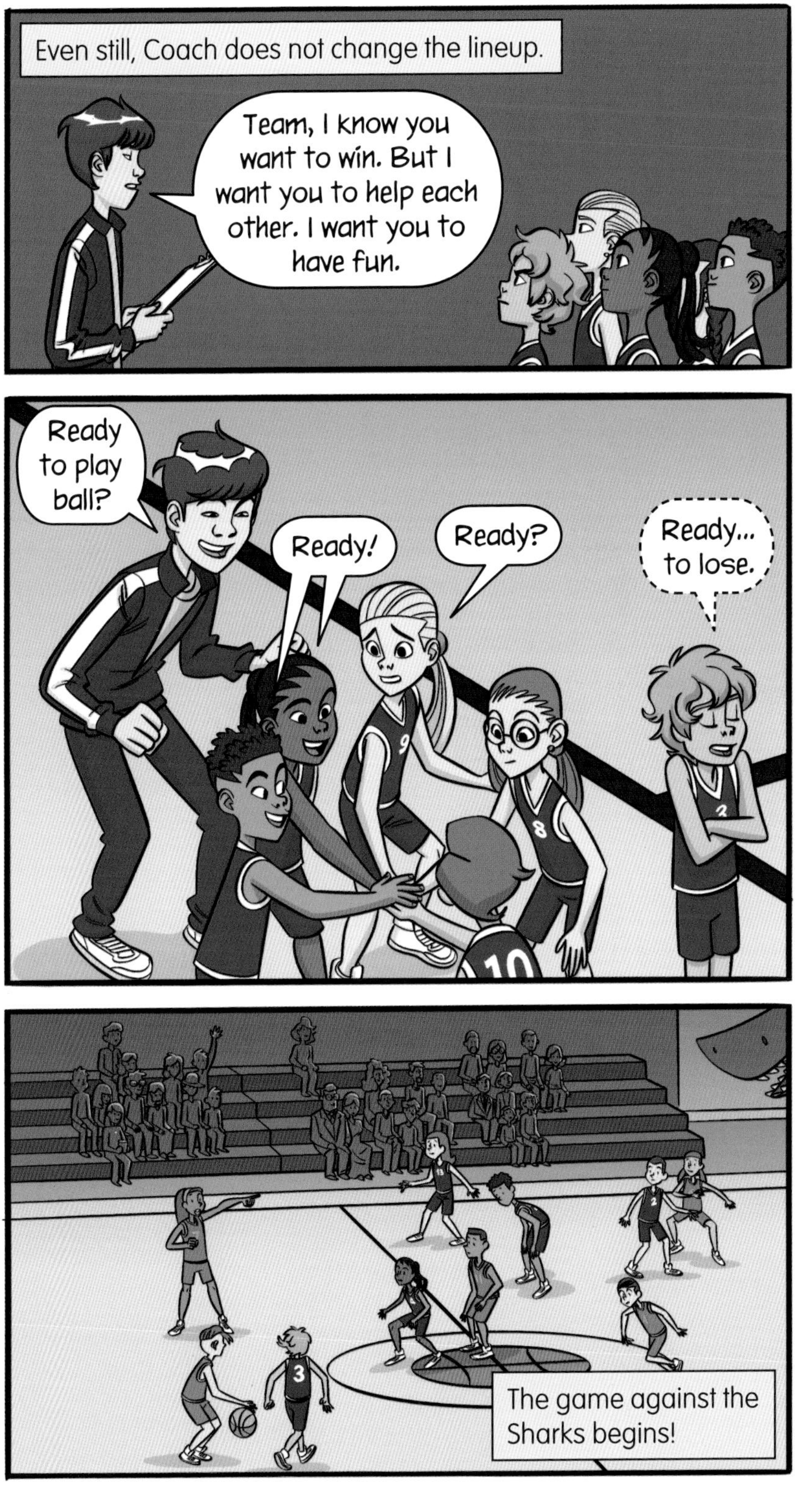
Even still, Coach does not change the lineup.
Team, I know you want to win. But I want you to help each other. I want you to have fun.
Ready to play ball?
Ready!
Ready?
Ready... to lose.
The game against the Sharks begins!

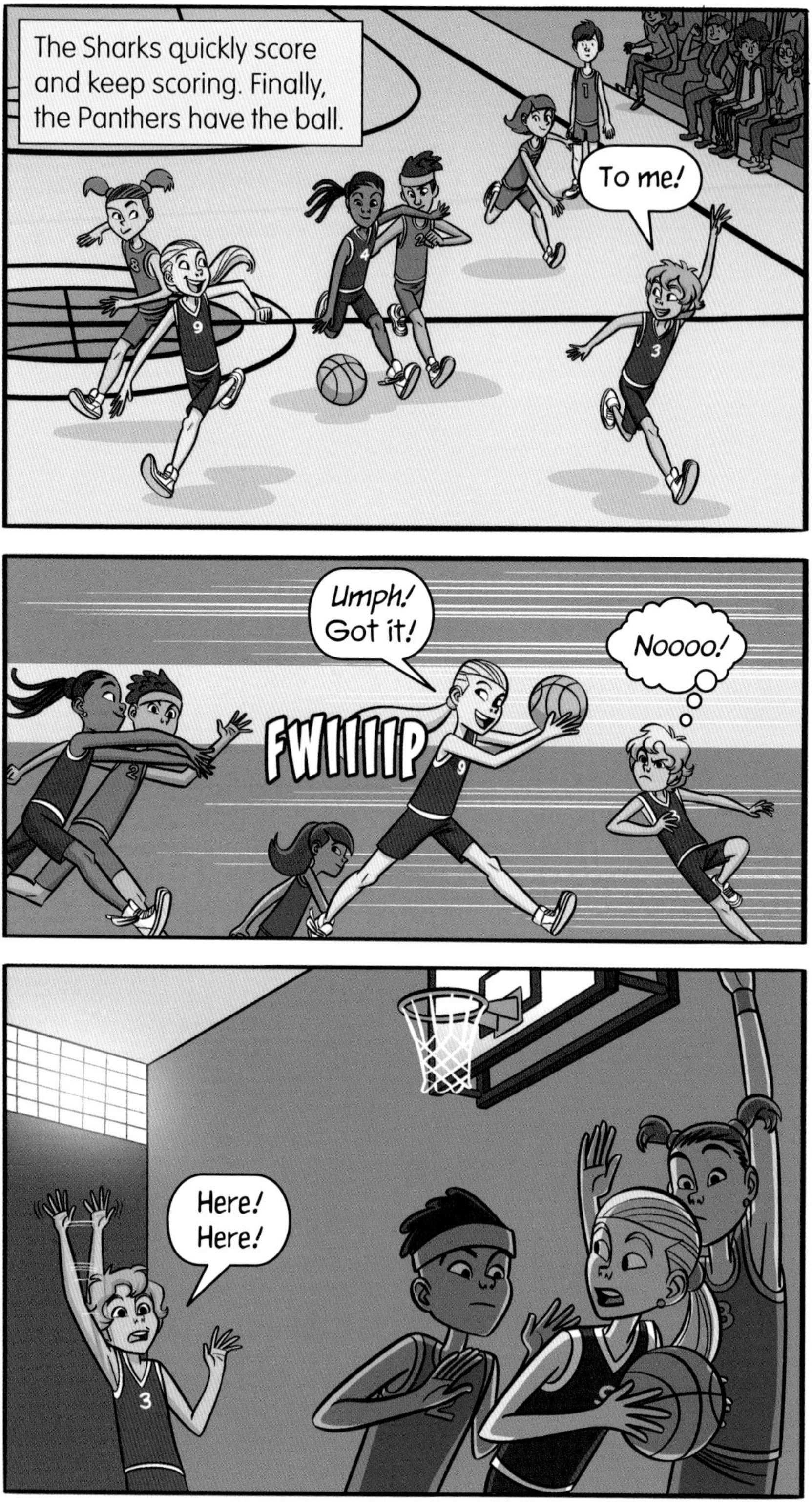
The Sharks quickly score and keep scoring. Finally, the Panthers have the ball.
To me!
Umph! Got it!
Noooo!
FWIIIIP
Here! Here!

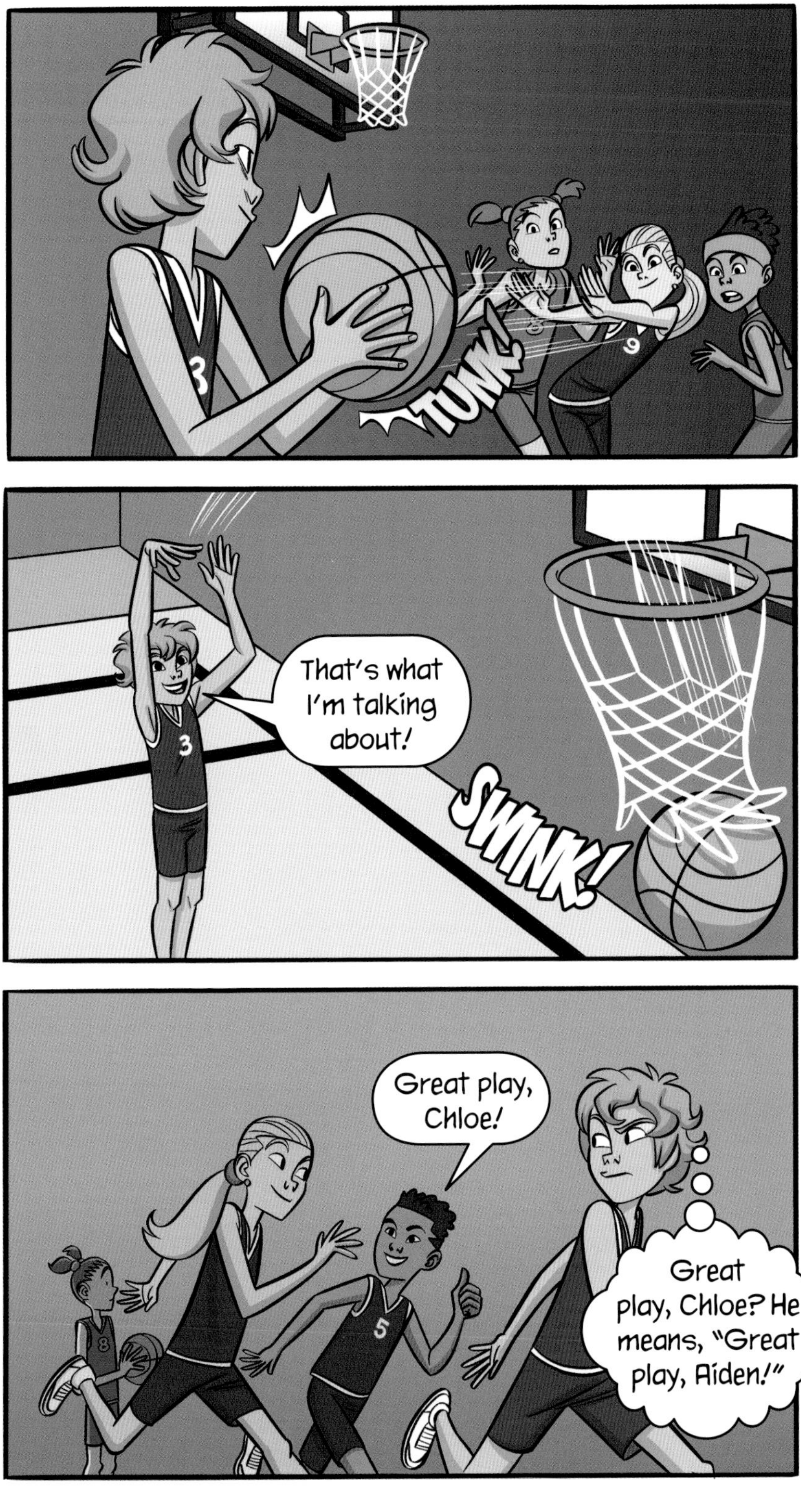
TUNK!
That's what I'm talking about!
SWINK!
Great play, Chloe!
Great play, Chloe? He means, "Great play, Aiden!"

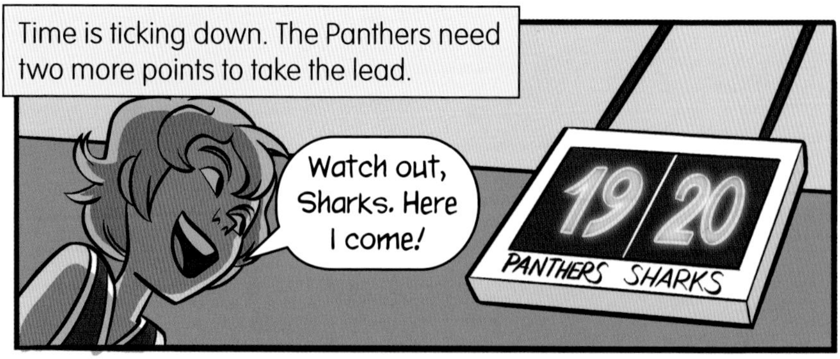
Time is ticking down. The Panthers need two more points to take the lead.
Watch out, Sharks. Here I come!
19 20
PANTHERS SHARKS

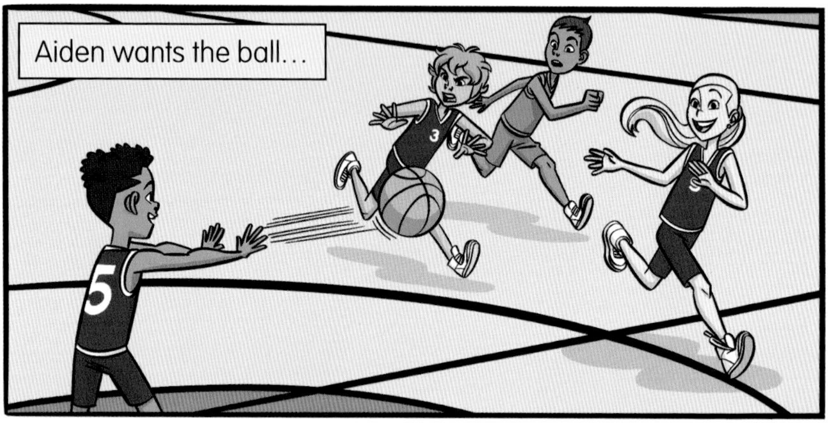
Aiden wants the ball…
5
3

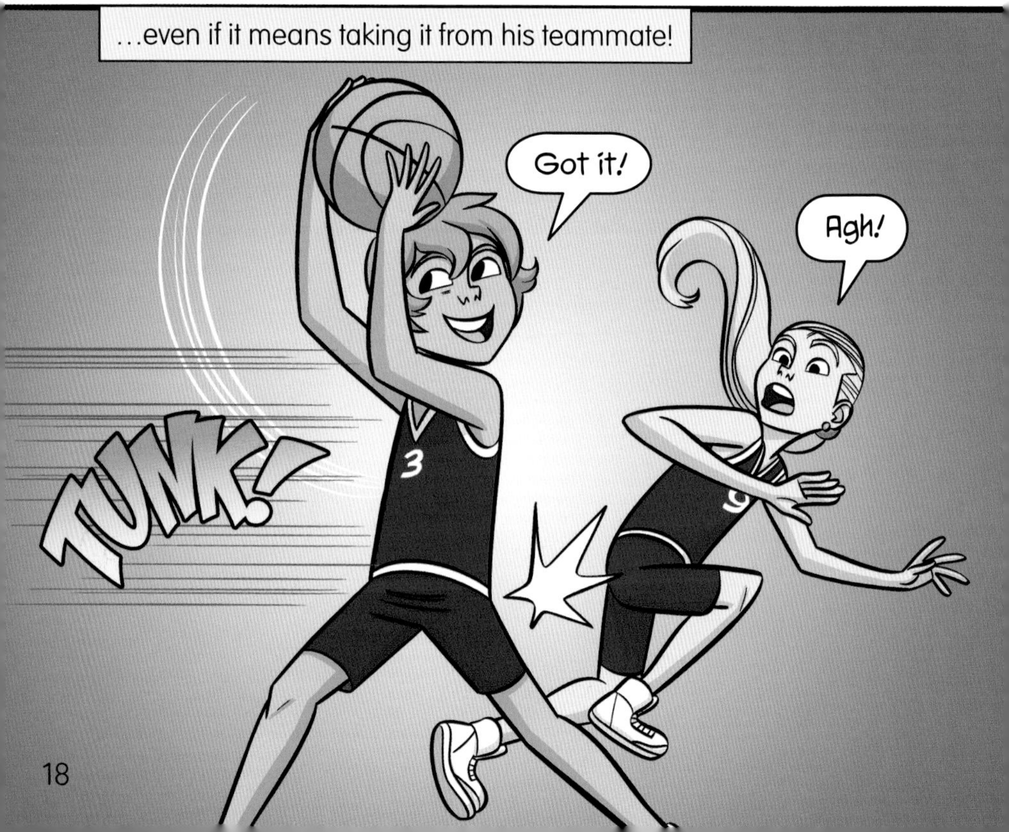
…even if it means taking it from his teammate!
Got it!
Agh!
TUNK!
3

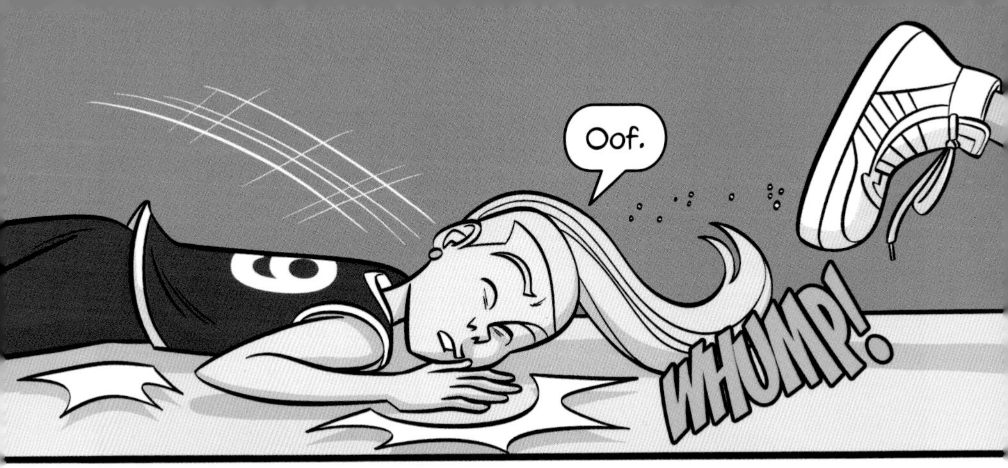
Oof.
WHUMP!

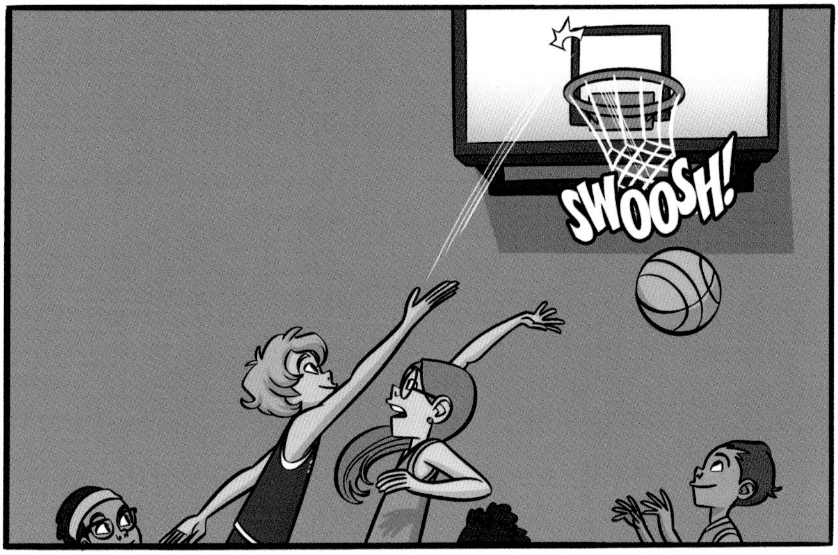
SWOOSH!

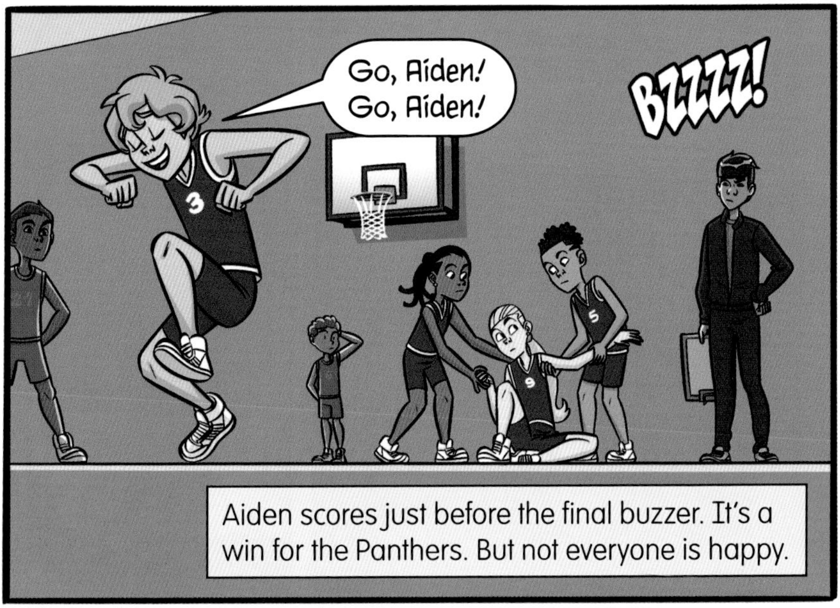
Go, Aiden!
Go, Aiden!
BZZZZ!
Aiden scores just before the final buzzer. It's a win for the Panthers. But not everyone is happy.

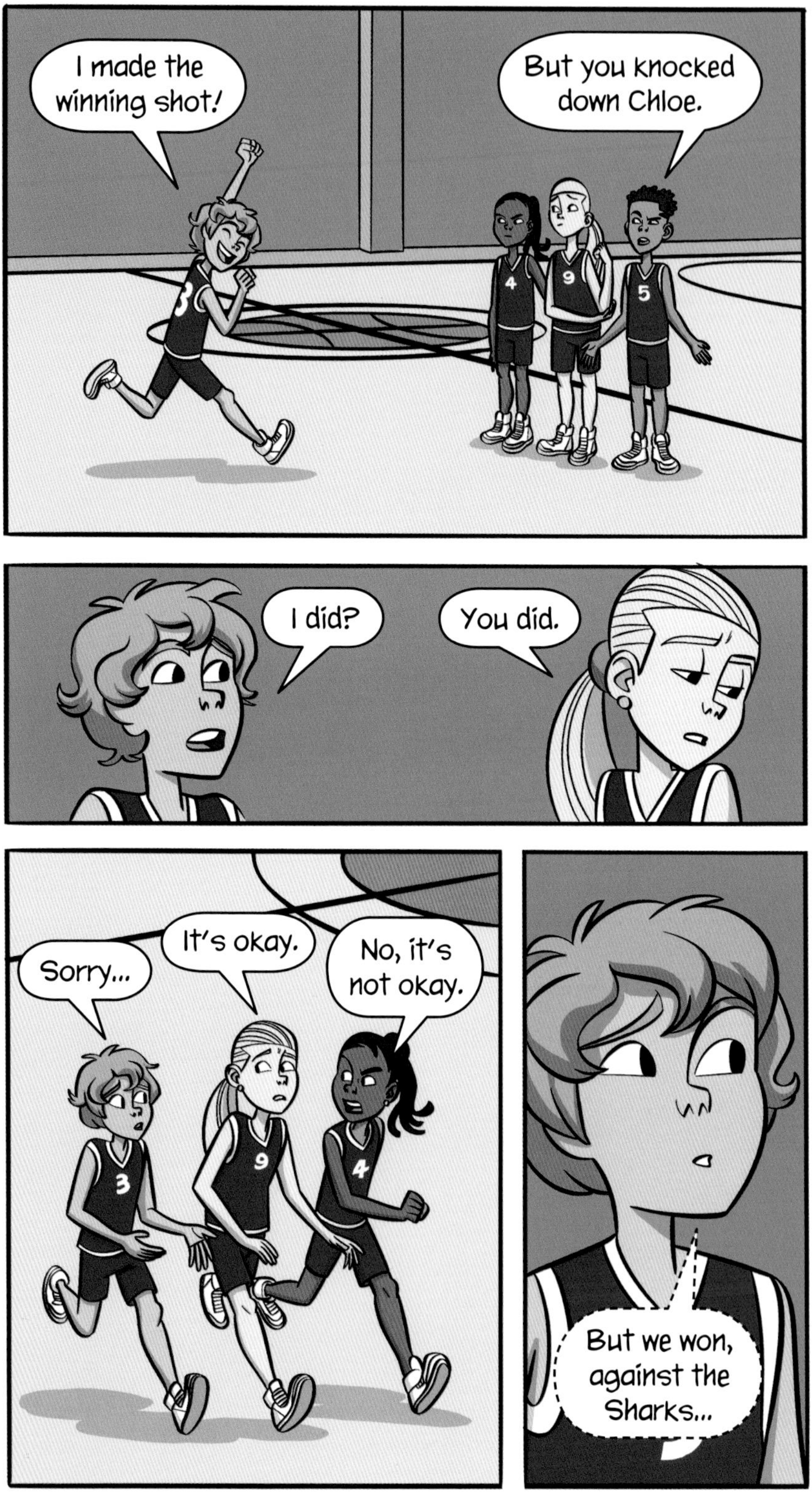
I made the winning shot!
But you knocked down Chloe.
I did?
You did.
Sorry...
It's okay.
No, it's not okay.
But we won, against the Sharks...

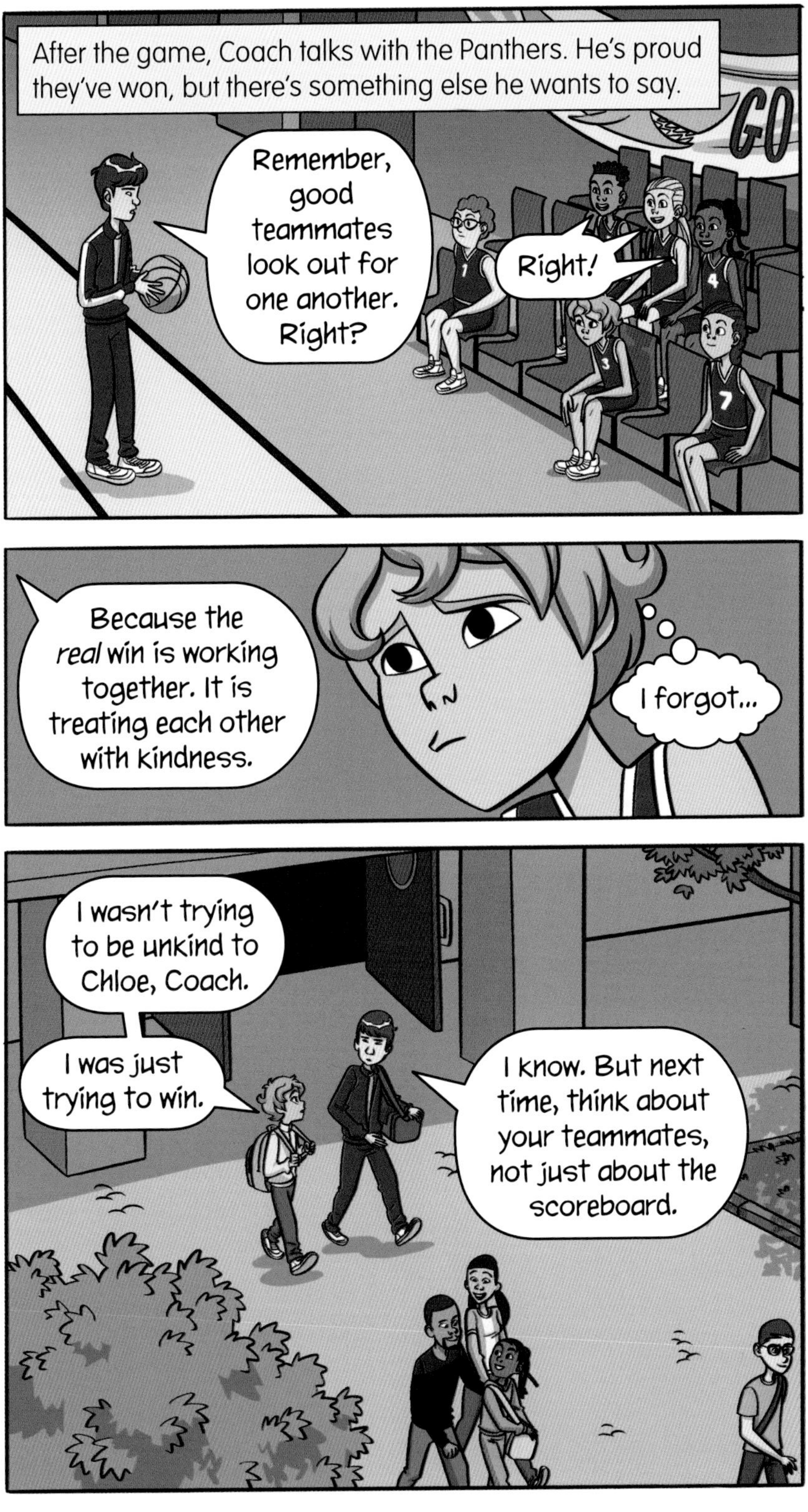
After the game, Coach talks with the Panthers. He's proud they've won, but there's something else he wants to say.
GO
Remember, good teammates look out for one another. Right?
Right!
Because the *real* win is working together. It is treating each other with kindness.
I forgot...
I wasn't trying to be unkind to Chloe, Coach.
I was just trying to win.
I know. But next time, think about your teammates, not just about the scoreboard.

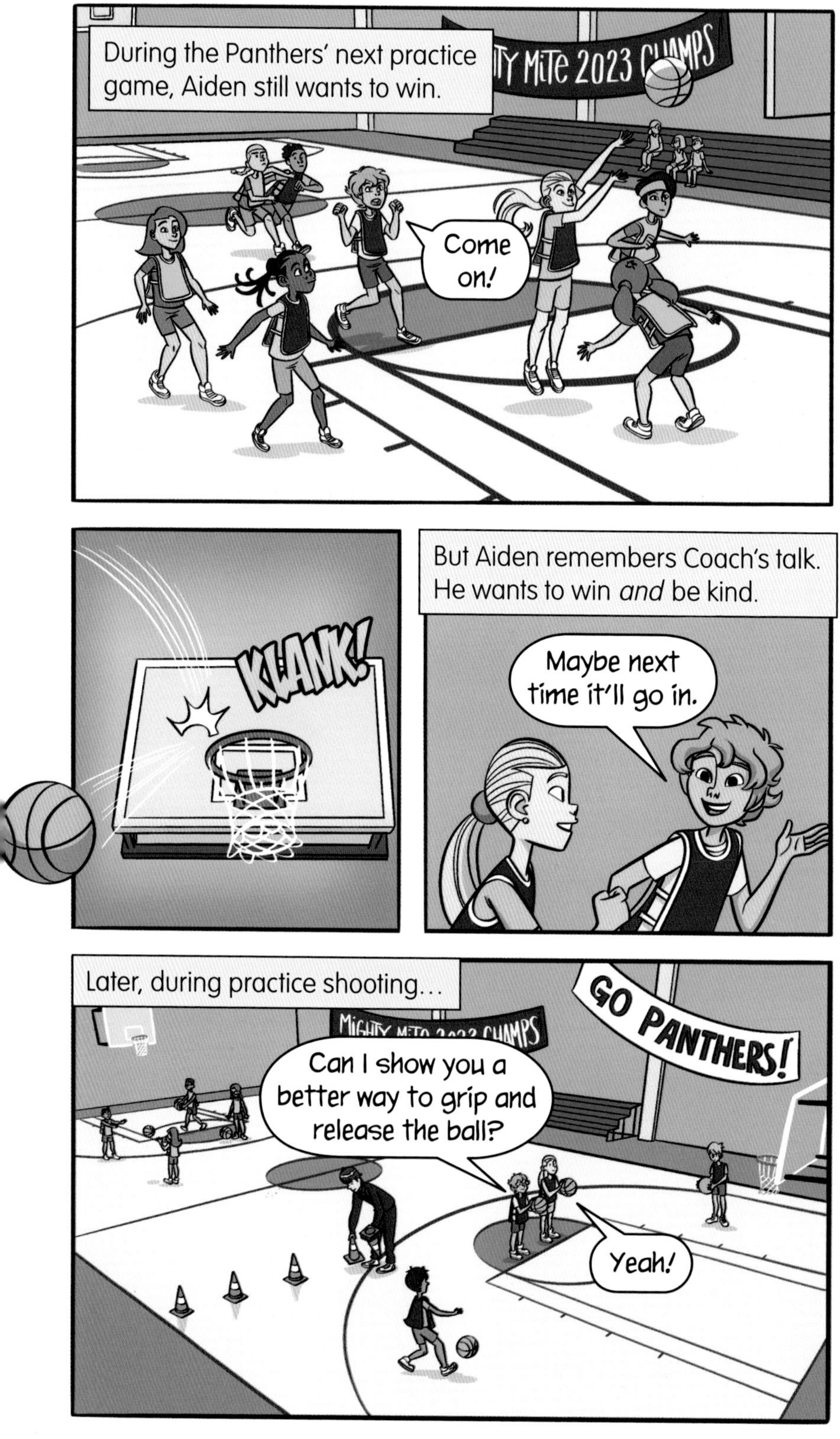
During the Panthers' next practice game, Aiden still wants to win.
Come on!
KLANK!
But Aiden remembers Coach's talk. He wants to win *and* be kind.
Maybe next time it'll go in.
Later, during practice shooting…
GO PANTHERS!
Can I show you a better way to grip and release the ball?
Yeah!

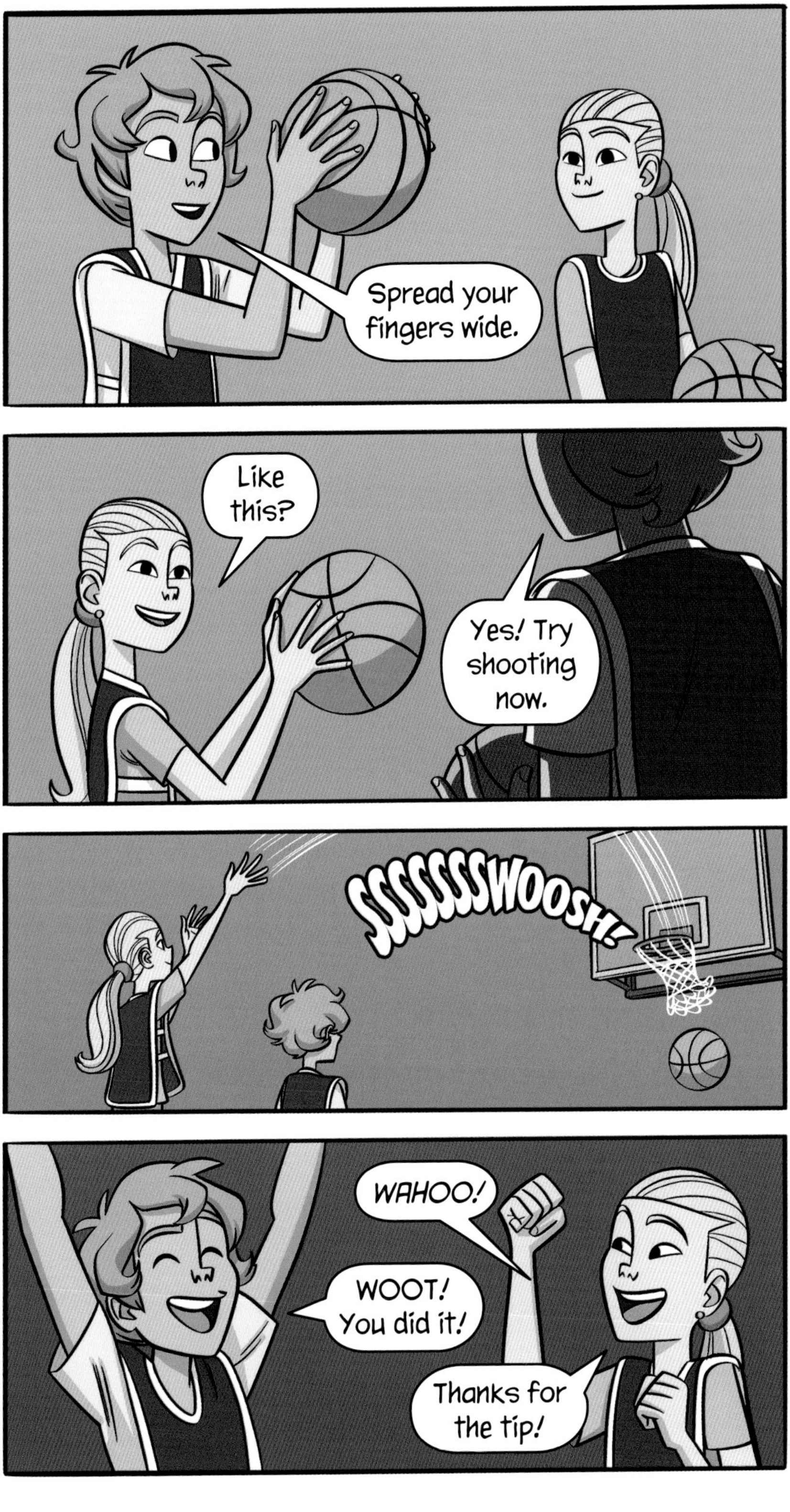
Spread your fingers wide.
Like this?
Yes! Try shooting now.
SSSSSSWOOSH!
WAHOO!
WOOT! You did it!
Thanks for the tip!

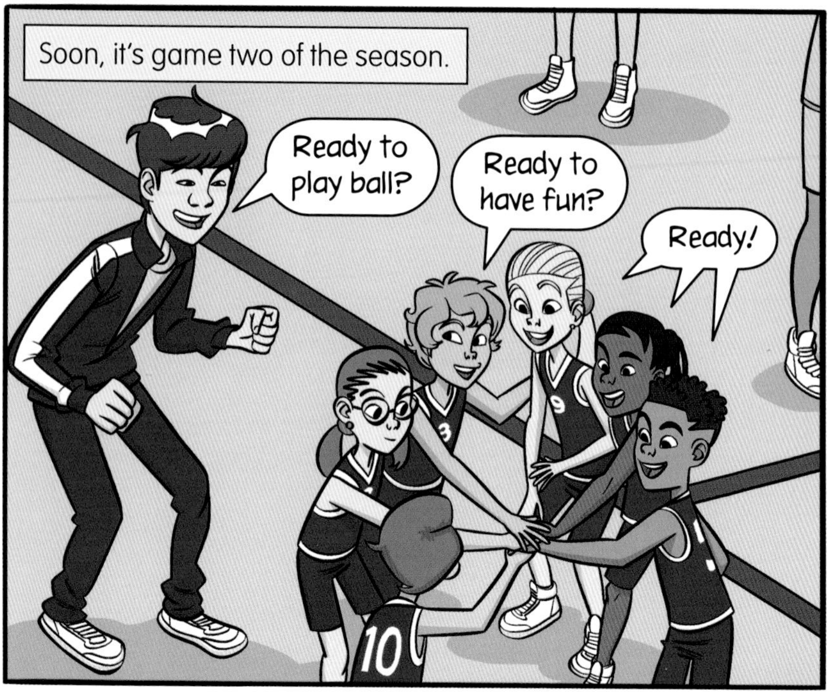
Soon, it's game two of the season.
Ready to play ball?
Ready to have fun?
Ready!
10

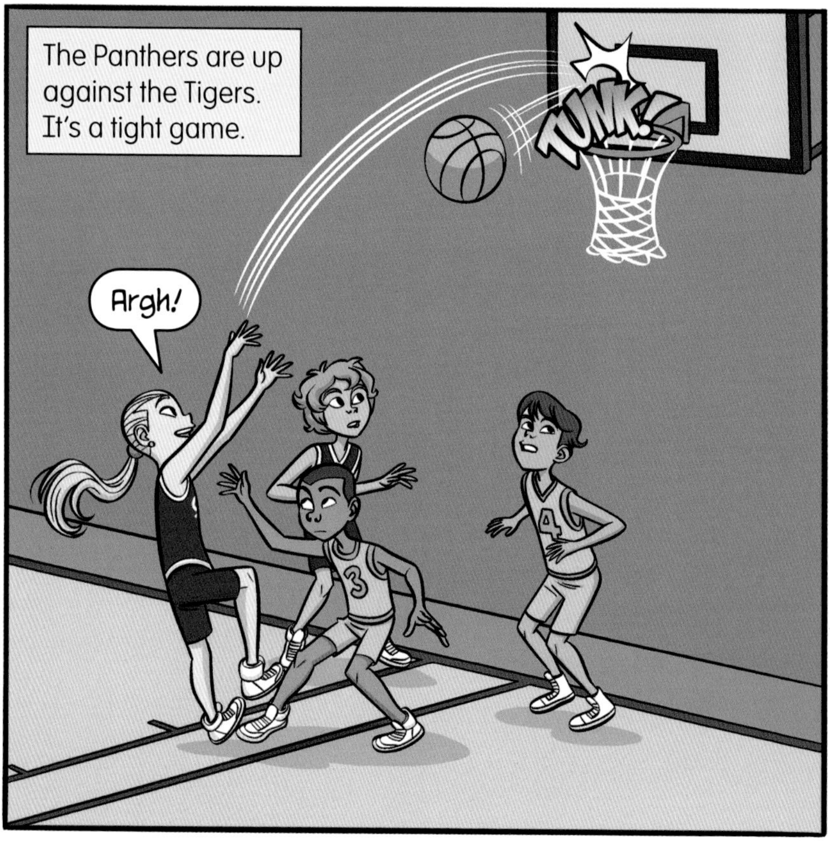
The Panthers are up against the Tigers. It's a tight game.
TUNK!
Argh!

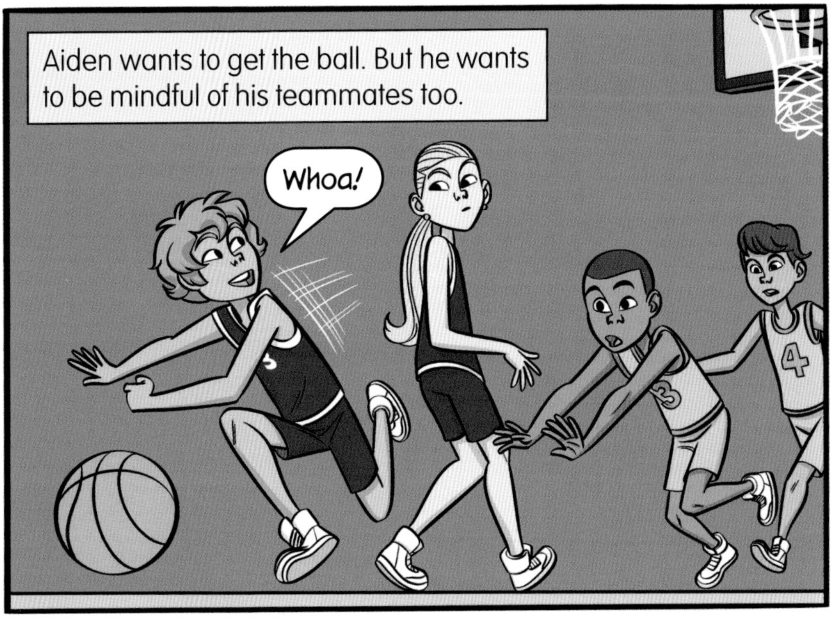
Aiden wants to get the ball. But he wants to be mindful of his teammates too.
Whoa!

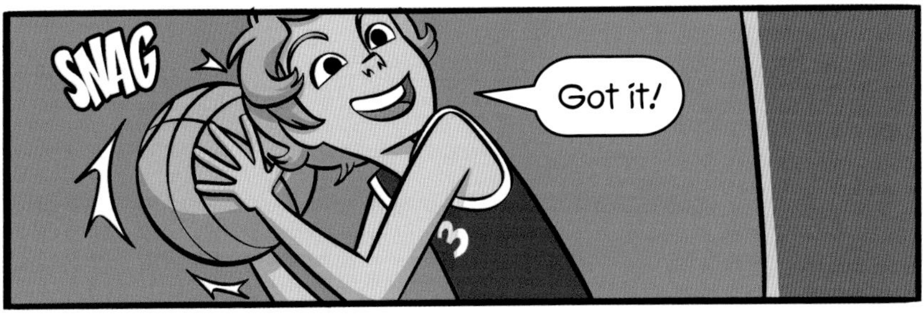
SNAG
Got it!

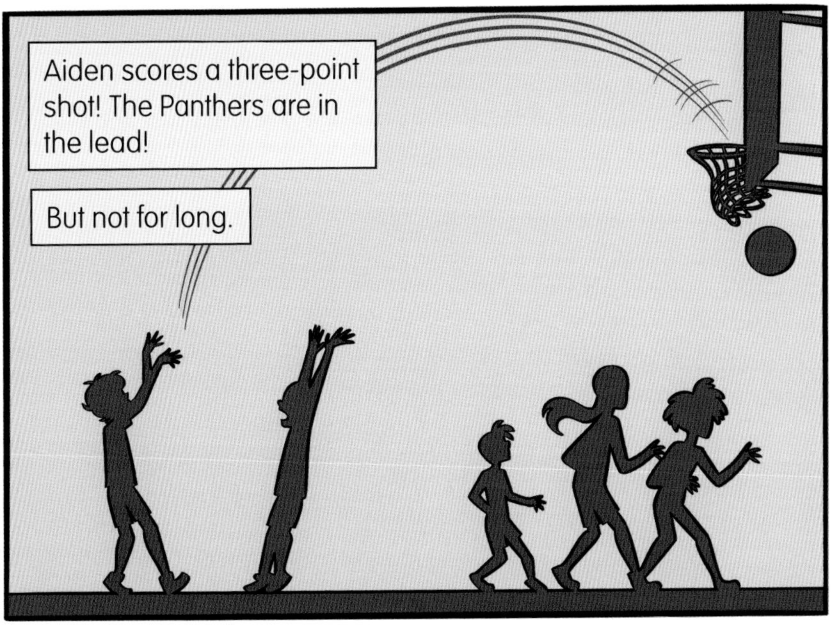
Aiden scores a three-point shot! The Panthers are in the lead!
But not for long.

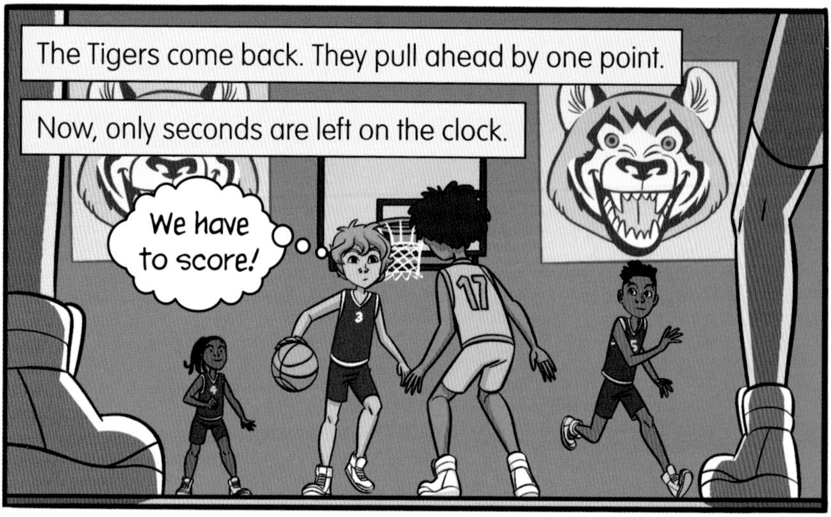
The Tigers come back. They pull ahead by one point.
Now, only seconds are left on the clock.
We have to score!

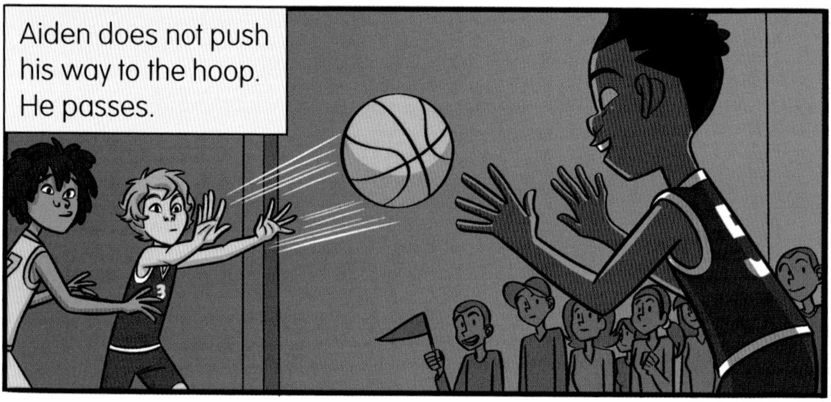
Aiden does not push his way to the hoop. He passes.

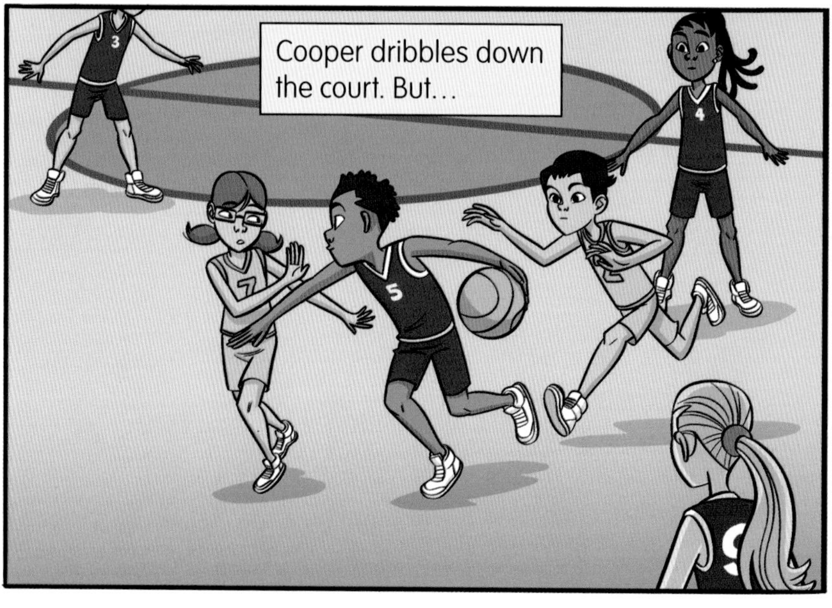
Cooper dribbles down the court. But…

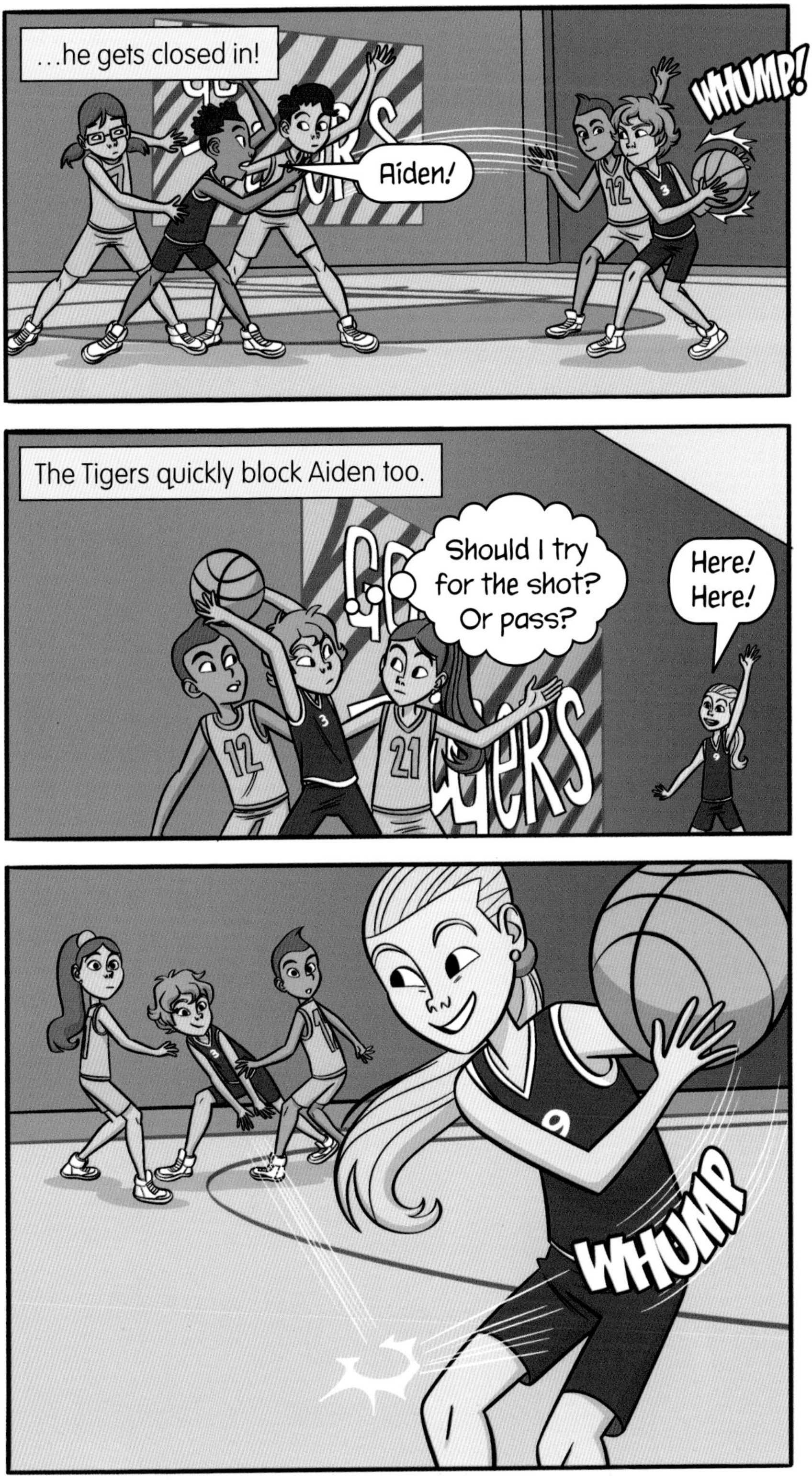
...he gets closed in!
Aiden!
WHUMP!
The Tigers quickly block Aiden too.
Should I try for the shot? Or pass?
Here! Here!
WHUMP

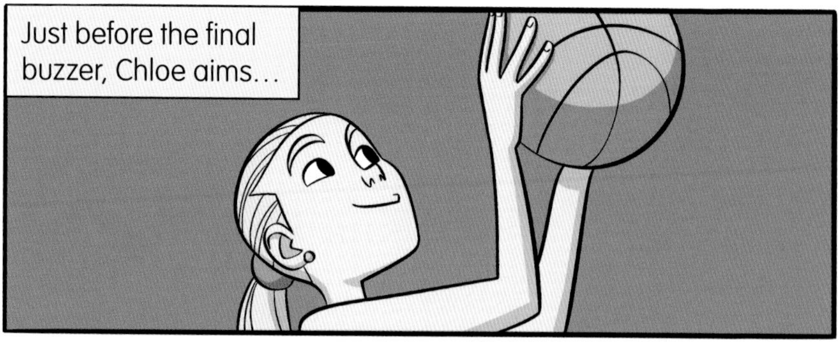
Just before the final buzzer, Chloe aims...

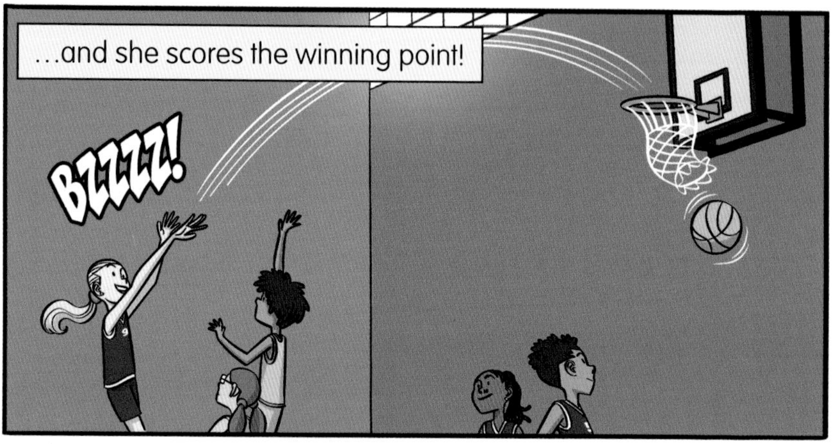
...and she scores the winning point!
BZZZZZ!

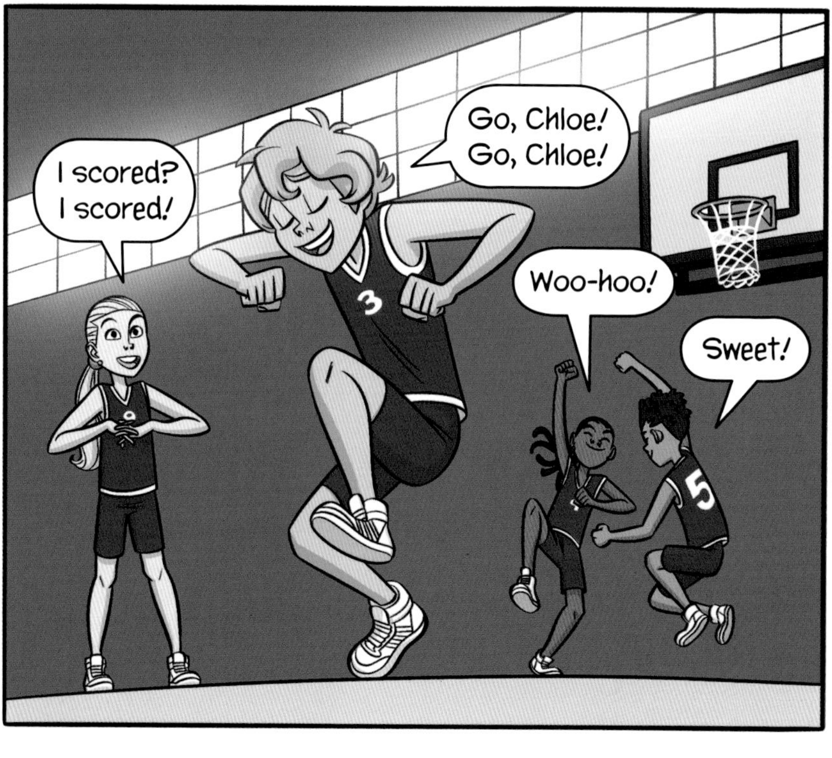
I scored? I scored!
Go, Chloe! Go, Chloe!
Woo-hoo!
Sweet!

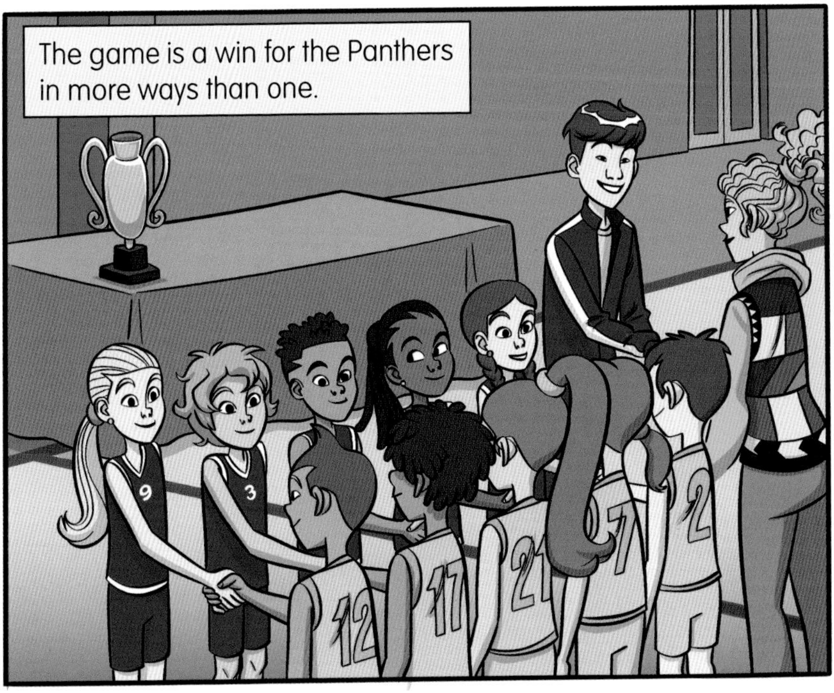
The game is a win for the Panthers in more ways than one.

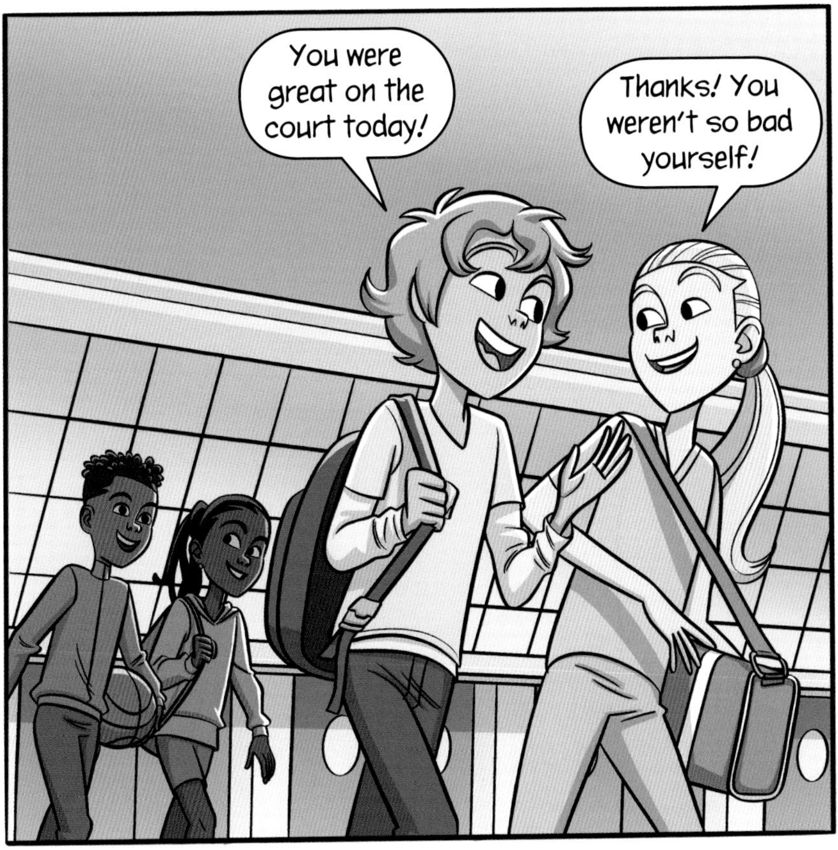
You were great on the court today!
Thanks! You weren't so bad yourself!

TALK ABOUT IT

1. Coach said that working together and being kind are better than winning. Do you agree? Why or why not?

2. In your own words, describe how Aiden first felt about Chloe joining the team. What in the art and text makes you think that?

3. Cooper and Lyra spoke up when Aiden was being unkind to Chloe. Do you find it easy or difficult to speak up when a friend is unkind? What can help you to be brave like Cooper and Lyra?

WRITE ABOUT IT

1. With an adult's help, view a coaching tip about properly shooting a basketball. Write a how-to list that would be easy for a new player to follow.

2. Imagine you are Aiden. Write a poem describing how it feels when you are dribbling or scoring.

3. Pretend you are a reporter for the school newspaper. You watched the game between the Panthers and the Tigers. Write an article that describes how the game went. Draw a "photograph" to go with the article.

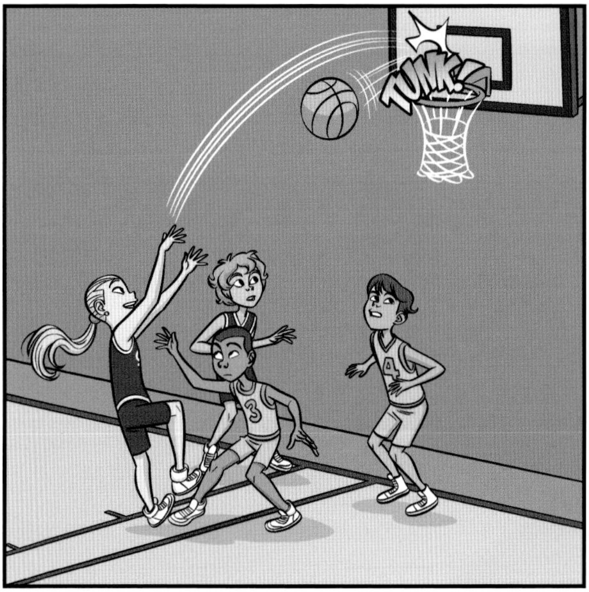

TUNK!

ABOUT THE WRITER

Dionna L. Mann is a children's book author and freelance journalist. She spent more than 25 years volunteering and working in the school system where her talented now-grown children attended. As a person of color, she enjoys learning about lesser-known people found in the records of African American history. One day she hopes to swim with dolphins. Find her online at dionnalmann.com.

ABOUT THE ARTIST

Oscar Herrero was born in Madrid, Spain, and studied journalism before deciding to devote himself entirely to art. He is an illustrator, character designer, and writer with experience in illustrating children's books, comics, magazine covers, album cover art, and video games, as well as working as a visual development artist for leading animation studios.